A DAY IN THE LIFE OF
OSCAR THE GROUCH

Featuring Jim Henson's Sesame Street Muppets
by LINDA HAYWARD · Illustrated by BILL DAVIS

A SESAME STREET / GOLDEN PRESS BOOK
Published by Western Publishing Company, Inc.
in conjunction with Children's Television Workshop.

© 1981 Children's Television Workshop. Muppet characters © 1981 Muppets, Inc. All rights reserved. Printed in U.S.A. SESAME STREET® and the SESAME STREET SIGN are trademarks and service marks of Children's Television Workshop. GOLDEN®, GOLDEN BOOKS® and GOLDEN PRESS® are trademarks of Western Publishing Company, Inc. No part of this book may be reproduced or copied in any form without written permission from the publisher. Library of Congress Catalog Card Number: 81-83507 ISBN 0-307-11611-5 / ISBN 0-307-61611-8 (lib. bdg.)

My name is Oscar the Grouch and this is the street where I live. I bet you think that being a grouch on Sesame Street is a lot of fun. Well, let me tell you something. A day on Sesame Street is just like any day on any other street.

BUMP! BUMP! BUMP! At six o'clock every morning the newspaper carrier delivers newspapers to the building next to my can. What a terrible noise to wake up to. I love it. It's that BUMP! BUMP! BUMP! that gets me off to a nice grouchy start every morning.

At seven o'clock in the morning I eat breakfast. Today I'm having orange rinds, rotten eggs, burned bacon, and stale bread crumbs. What a great meal! But I'm sure the breakfast at your house is just as good.

Oh, no! Here come my neighbors to get their papers.
"Good morning, Oscar!" says Ernie.
"Good morning, Oscar!" says Grover.
"Good morning, Oscar!" says Prairie Dawn.
AAGGH! Even burned bacon tastes bad after three
GOOD MORNINGS in a row.

Eight o'clock in the morning is one of those
nice times in the day when a grouch can really relax.
Everyone is hurrying to school or to work. Rush,
rush, rush! No one has time to stop and say hello.

Isn't it wonderful?

The mail carrier comes at nine o'clock. Today she delivers four letters to the Count. Once again, there is no mail for me. So who wants a silly old letter, anyhow?

Ten o'clock in the morning is clean-up time on Sesame Street. Big Bird starts sweeping and dusting and dusting and sweeping.

I can't stand clean-up time. I keep thinking, "There goes another great collection of trash."

At eleven o'clock in the morning some of
the people around here do chores and errands.

Bert does his laundry
at the laundromat.

Biff takes his paycheck to the bank.

Rodeo Rosie picks up
her cleaning at the cleaners.

And what about me?
Well, my favorite chore is
waiting for the Mudman's
delivery. Heh heh heh.

It's twelve o'clock noon, and that's lunch time. I don't know about your neighborhood, but on Sesame Street friends share their lunches. But grouches don't share. I would hate to part with any of my delicious peanut butter and sardine sandwich.

At one o'clock, right after lunch, it's nap time. Even Barkley takes a nap. I just happen to like to play my trombone at one o'clock in the afternoon. Can I help it if Barkley doesn't appreciate great trombone playing?

At two o'clock in the afternoon a lot of people go to the park. There's just one thing I don't understand. The joggers and walkers and bird watchers and kite flyers like to visit the park on a nice sunny day.

I only go to the park when it rains.

By three o'clock in the afternoon most of the kids are home from school and playing games. They're all doing things they like to do.

Around this time I do something I like to do, too. I complain.

"Hey, Barkley, cut that out! Hey, Prairie Dawn,
there's too much shouting! Hey, Ernie, stop laughing!"
We grouches don't like to see anyone having a
good time.

At four o'clock on Tuesday the bookmobile comes
to Sesame Street. Well, it is now four o'clock on Tuesday
and that is why I am standing in a line in this crowded
bookmobile. I am waiting to check out my favorite book—
Mother Grouch Rhymes.

At last! My favorite time of day! Rush hour!

At five o'clock in the afternoon everyone who has been somewhere else working all day begins rushing home. Cars are stuck in traffic. People are tired and hungry. Motors are rumbling. Tummies are grumbling. Even cheerful people are a little bit grouchy.

Isn't it wonderful?

At six o'clock in the evening I eat my supper. I suppose you eat your supper in the evening, too.

Tonight I am having pizza. Now I ask you, is there anything more delicious than pizza with banana slices on top?

At seven o'clock in the evening Ernie takes his bath.

Here at Oscar's can it's also bathtime, but not for me.
Slimey, my pet worm, takes his bath at seven o'clock, too.
Of course, he takes a mud bath. Heh heh heh.

At eight o'clock it's storytime. Over at Big Bird's nest Big Bird reads to all the little birds. They just love a good book. Personally, I can't stand happy endings.

Whew! Now it's bedtime—nine o'clock. Everybody turns out the lights. Everybody snuggles into bed. At last— peace and quiet.

Now it is time for me to practice my trombone again.

What a perfect ending to another yucchy day on Sesame Street.

ABCDEFGHIJ